FAITH 101:

NOW, Faith IS!

Angela J. Walker

Copyright © 2019   Angela J. Walker

All rights reserved.

ISBN: 9781700999610 (soft cover)

No part of this publication may be reproduced, stored in a retrieval system, or transmitted in any form or by any means-electronic, mechanical, photocopy, recording, or any other, except for brief quotations in printed reviews, without the prior written permission of the author.

Unless otherwise noted, all Scripture quotations are from the King James Version of the Bible.

Scripture quotations marked (AMPC) are from The Amplified Bible. Old Testament @ 1965, 1987 by the Zondervan Corporation. The Amplified New Testament @ 1958, 1987 by the Lockman Foundation

Scripture quotations marked (MSG) are from The Message. Copyright @ 1993, 1995 by Eugene H. Peterson.

Scripture quotations marked (NLT) are from The New Living Translation copyright @ 1996, 2004. Used by permission of Tyndale House Publishers, Inc. Wheaton, Illinois.

Scripture quotations marked (NIV) are from The Holy Bible, New International Version copyright @ 1973, 1978, 1984. By International Bible Society.

CONTENTS

DEDICATION

I give glory and honor to my Lord and Savior Jesus Christ, who is the head of my life. To my husband of 33 years, Pastor Perry Walker, Sr. You are the love of my youth, my life partner. I thank God for you. To my children, Perry Jr., Charity and Micah (Kaylah), I love each one of you more than anything in this world. To my grandchildren Madison and Malachi, you both have increased my capacity to receive love. You all continually motivate and inspire me to never give up, to press on, and to succeed. To ALL those who have stood with me and believed in the call of God over my life. Thank you! My loving church family, Deliverance Family Worship Center, I honor you all. To my sisters Linda and Shirley (Stafford, VA), I am thankful for the unfailing love, continual encouragement and support you both give me as I write each book. My dear friend Ashley Sutton, I treasure you and thank you for holding my hand as I labored to birth Faith 101. I also want to honor and thank my spiritual parents, Pastors Michael and Kennetha Moore (Faith Chapel/Birmingham, AL).

FOREWORD

Romans 10:17 KJV "So then faith cometh by hearing, and hearing by the word of God"

I struggled with the decision to write this book. I asked myself am I qualified to write about faith? What are my faith credentials? In April 2017, I began studying about faith. The more I studied, the greater my faith grew. Through the direction and inspiration of the Holy Spirit, I am exercising my faith through obedience, as I write this book. My heart's desire is to encourage and strengthen everyone who reads Faith 101 in their faith walk. The more you read, study, and hear about faith, the more confident you will become in exercising your faith. For those of you who believe God has called you to something bigger and greater than what you are able to accomplish within your own strength, I am writing to you. I want you to know God is faithful. He will perform every promise He has ever spoken to you through His Word. I believe in you. My sisters and brothers don't give up. Keep believing. Stay in faith. You got this! It's just a matter of time before others see the manifestation of what you have been believing all along. Your life is the representation of Faith 101: Now, Faith IS!

CHAPTER ONE

BACK TO BASICS: SAVED BY FAITH

Romans 10:9-10 KJV "That if thou shalt confess with thy mouth the Lord Jesus, and shalt believe in thine heart that God hath raised him from the dead, thou shalt be saved. For with the heart man believeth unto righteousness; and with the mouth confession is made unto salvation."

Most of us can recall when we accepted Jesus Christ as Lord and Savior or as some call it, got saved. This was the day the trajectory of our lives were changed forever. We may not be able to remember the exact date but we most should definitely have fond memories of the experience. We are all saved by faith. Our accepting Jesus Christ as Lord and Savior was the foundation or basis on which our entire Christian lives are constructed. We need to understand this, because as believers, everything else will be built or founded layer by layer, on our salvation experience. If we do not understand the role our faith played in the creation of our spiritual lives, we will never be able to advance from hoping to living faith-filled lives.

Accepting Jesus into our hearts was our first exercise of faith. All believers have this in common. Salvation can only be obtained by faith in Jesus Christ. God is a spirit. We cannot accept or engage Him through our flesh or natural man. We must accept Him into our hearts and communicate with Him continually and consistently through our spiritual selves in faith. We may have different salvation experiences but the method by which we received salvation is universal for all our brothers and sisters in Christ.

Hebrews 11:6 KJV "But without faith it is impossible to please him: for he that cometh to God must believe that he is, and that is he is a rewarder of them that diligently seek him."

God purposed and designed our introductory experience in walking by faith to be established through our receiving Jesus as Lord and Savior. This act of faith laid the groundwork or foundation for all future interactions with Him. God wants us to understand by this experience that faith is mandatory for our relationship with Him. The salvation experience was designed to demonstrate to us that we must continuously operate in faith throughout our entire lives here on earth. Just as we acquired salvation through faith, we will also have to exercise our faith continually in order to receive all the other promises of God.

Hebrews 10:38 KJV *"Now the just shall live by faith: but if any man draw back, my soul shall have no pleasure in him."*

God desires that we all receive salvation. Salvation cannot be obtained without an exercise of faith. We could not have gotten saved without believing He would save us. We did not call on the name of the Lord without first believing He existed. Salvation is available to everyone who in faith calls on the name of Jesus Christ. Everyone will have an opportunity to accept Christ, however; some won't because they will not believe the gospel. God loves us all. He is not a respecter of persons. His desire is that none should perish. The process of salvation is the same for each of us. It is no harder or easier for your neighbor than it was for you to receive Him. We receive Him by faith.

Romans 10:13 KJV "For whosoever shall call upon the name of the Lord shall be saved."

Salvation is obtained by hearing the gospel or good news of the saving power of Jesus Christ. Confessing with our mouths and believing in our hearts that God raised Him from the dead. Salvation is a spiritual reality that cannot be understood with a carnal or natural mindset. To the natural man, it does not make sense. Accepting Jesus Christ as Lord and Savior is a simple process that can only be accomplished by our willingness to believe scripture. The Bible is not just a well-written book. The Bible is the Word of God.

Accepting the Word of God or the Bible by faith keeps us from overcomplicating or trying to analyze salvation by attempting to intellectually reason or understand exactly how it works. We believe by faith all scripture is God-inspired and is the foundation for faith in every area of our lives. *2 Timothy 3:16a KJV "All scripture is given by inspiration of God".* There is no other way to obtain salvation than believing and having faith in the Word of God.

Hebrews 11:6 KJV "But without faith it is impossible to please him: for he that cometh to God must believe that he is, and that he is a rewarder of them that diligently seek him."

Let's look at our salvation process. We believe Adam's disobedience or sin, in the Garden of Eden, resulted in all mankind being borne in or made into sinners. We believe we became lost or disconnected from God because of Adam's actions. Sin separates us from God as a result of disobedience. We may not exactly grasp how it all came about, nevertheless; we must accept this as truth. We needed a Savior. We must accept through one man, Adam's disobedience we all became sinners. We are now able to understand and accept our need for salvation through Jesus Christ, which could only be purchased for us by His death on the cross.

Romans 5:18-20 AMPC "Well then, as one man's trespass [one man's false step and falling away led] to condemnation for all men, so one Man's act of righteousness [leads] to acquittal and right standing with God and life for all men. For just as by one man's disobedience (failing to hear, [a]heedlessness, and carelessness) the many were constituted sinners, so by one Man's obedience the many will be constituted righteous (made acceptable to God, brought into right standing with Him). But then Law came in, [only] to expand and increase the trespass [making it more apparent and exciting opposition]. But where sin increased and abounded, grace (God's unmerited favor) has surpassed it and increased the more and superabounded,"

We were indeed sinners in need of a Savior. Jesus was a righteous and greater man. His death resulted in our being made righteous. For everyone who believes in

Christ, His death paid the penalty for all our sins; past, present and future. His death for the believer has put us back in right standing with the Father. We understood we acquired salvation through faith in Christ's birth, death, and resurrection. Most of us don't resist and struggle to understand that faith is necessary to receive salvation. We can exercise faith and believe the Word of God pertaining to this area.

Galatians 3:13-15 KJV "Christ hath redeemed us from the curse of the law, being made a curse for us: for it is written, Cursed is everyone that hangeth on a tree: That the blessing of Abraham might come on the Gentiles through Jesus Christ; that we might receive the promise of the Spirit through faith."

Regardless of how we try to understand it, in the natural, it will never fully make sense. We have confessed with our mouths and believed in our hearts God sent His only begotten son Jesus Christ, who we have never seen, to die for our sins over 2000 years ago on the cross. We had not yet been born, yet we believe His death paid

12

the penalty for all our past, present and future sin. We accept this as truth and as a result, we believe we are now saved. God wants us to understand as His children just as we had faith for salvation, the possibilities through faith are endless for us as His children. We were born-again as His heirs to walk in creative power if we believe. Salvation was never meant to be the target goal of our faith walk. It was designed to be the beginning.

Ephesians 2:8 AMPC "For it is by free grace (God's unmerited favor) that you are saved ([a]delivered from judgment and made partakers of Christ's salvation) through [your] faith. And this [salvation] is not of yourselves [of your own doing, it came not through your own striving], but it is the gift of God;"

We are all saved by grace through our faith in the death, burial, and resurrection of our Lord and Savior Jesus Christ. Our salvation was not earned, and we won't ever deserve to be saved. Salvation is a gift from God. God sent His son to die for us while we were yet sinners. He did not wait for us to get right or fix ourselves because we couldn't do so. God wanted us to experience the process of receiving by faith what we have not earned and what we do not deserve.

Satan constantly tries to challenge, discount and undermine this faith move because he understands the same way we received our salvation is the same way we will receive everything else we desire from God. We don't have to earn loving relationships, good health, or financial prosperity. They all were encompassed in the salvation package. It's a finished work. Jesus Christ is sitting at the right hand of the Father. He said it was finished. He is no longer working on our behalf. We must obtain by faith the blessings of God the same way we obtained our salvation. Selah!

Most of us will argue with you if you tried to challenge us concerning our salvation. We will not allow anyone else's opinion of our relationship with God to cause us to accept that we are not saved. We accept our salvation as a gift we did not earn, therefore we will not relinquish it when we mess up. Being saved means that much to us. After making our confession of faith, even if we are struggling in our daily walk of righteousness, we hold fast to our proclamation of salvation, and rightfully so.

We yet boldly proclaim we are saved, and we remain firm in this belief even when others doubt our relationship with God. We are confident we have met the requirement to obtain salvation. We have chosen to believe and exercise faith in the salvation process. This pleases God. He meant for this to be our introduction to the process of living by faith, not our conclusion.

Romans 3:22-24 AMPC "Namely, the righteousness of God which comes by believing with personal trust and confident reliance on Jesus Christ (the Messiah). [And it is meant] for all who believe. For there is no distinction, Since all have sinned and are falling short of the honor and glory [a]which God bestows and receives. [All] are justified and made upright and in right standing with God, freely and gratuitously by His grace (His unmerited favor and mercy), through the redemption which is [provided] in Christ Jesus"

If you do not know Jesus Christ as Lord and Savior, please say this prayer:

DEAR GOD, I KNOW THAT I AM A SINNER. I ASK FOR YOUR FORGIVENESS. I BELIEVE YOU SENT JESUS TO DIE FOR MY SINS. I BELIEVE YOU RAISED HIM FROM THE DEAD. I TURN FROM MY SINS AND ASK YOU BE MY GOD. I FOLLOW YOU FROM THIS DAY FORWARD IN JESUS NAME.

CHAPTER ONE FAITH NOTES

_____

_____

_____

_____

_____

_____

_____

_____

_____

_____

_____

_____

_____

_____

_____

_____

_____

_____

_____

_____

CHAPTER TWO

A LITTLE BIT OF FAITH

Romans 12:3 KJV "For I say, through the grace given unto me, to every man that is among you, not to think of himself more highly than he ought to think; but to think soberly, according as God hath dealt to every man the measure of faith."

We are not faithless! Our faith journey is not about us having enough faith or waiting for God to instill in us the required amount of faith necessary for us to navigate through life. It is also not about us waiting to experience the manifestation of whatever we are believing to receive from God as believers. The enemy of our faith, the devil wants us to minimize the powerfulness of our faith by suggesting we either lack faith or somehow, we are responsible for rendering our minute amount of faith inoperable. The amount of faith we have is not the problem. The issue for most believers is our lack of confidence in the amount of faith we already currently possess. Haven't you heard; a little bit of faith goes a long way.

We each are a spirit, we possess a soul, we occupy a body. We do not have to ask God for what He has already placed within us. God has already dealt to each of us the amount or measure of faith necessary to receive Him into our hearts and to begin our spiritual journeys here on earth. There is no place in scripture where believers are instructed to ask God for more faith. Scripture tells us to make our requests known to God in faith. We were created by God as spiritual beings. Our spiritual selves were created innately possessing faith. There is nothing we cannot accomplish with the amount of faith we already possess.

Yes, some believers possess great faith. This level of faith was not just given to them. Their faith has grown and matured into what we now visibly see and admire. They have great faith now because they have exercised the measure of faith they received at salvation. Over time their faith developed into great faith. We too can operate in great faith if we are willing to stop being spiritually lazy and begin exercising the level of faith we currently possess. We must be willing to stand in faith for a headache before we can believe God for healing from brain cancer.

Mark 16:17a "And these signs shall follow them that believe;"

It is the lack of revelation of the power contained in the faith we possess that hinders us from walking in the manifestation of God's Word in our daily lives. Signs only follow those who believe signs will follow them! The apostles asked Jesus for more faith. They believed their lack of faith was the cause of their lack of manifestation. Jesus did not give them more faith. He did not tell them that fasting and praying would increase their faith. He simply reminded them of the powerfulness of the power in the faith they already possessed. We do not need more faith. We need to exercise the faith we already have.

Luke 17:5-6 KJV "And the apostles said unto the Lord, Increase our faith. And the Lord said, If ye had faith as a grain of mustard seed, ye might say unto this sycamine tree, Be thou plucked up by the root, and be thou planted in the sea; and it should obey you."

Faith is not about us; it is about God. Faith is based on God's ability, not on our ability. Faith must be established on the Word of God. If we cannot find what we are believing for in the Word of God, we are not standing in faith. Faith in God has no limitations. The amount of faith we have is not the issue. The awareness of the power in our faith is. Faith is not given to the deserving and withheld from the undeserving. Faith is a gift given to each one of us by our loving Father God. Faith was not given to us because we deserved it in any way. We did not earn it. Therefore, we cannot boast in our possessing great faith.   Faith was not meant to make us think more highly of ourselves than we should.

St. John 4:24 KJV "God is a spirit: and they that worship him must worship him in spirit and in truth."

The faith we possess operates because of our awareness of God's love for us, not because of our love for God. God's purpose and design for all of us being born with faith was so that we would be equipped with the capacity to accept Jesus Christ as our personal Lord and Savior. God's love empowers us to live faith-filled lives here on earth. Operating in faith is the only way our spirit can engage and interact with our heavenly Father. Operating in faith is how our spirit communes with the Father. No exercise of faith equals no fellowship with God. It is impossible to fellowship with a spiritual God through physical or natural means.

Ephesians 4:5-6 KJV "One Lord, one faith, one baptism, One God and Father of all, who is above all, and through all, and in you all."

There is only one faith. This means the faith that others are operating in is not more effective or of a different quality than what we have been given. All faith originates from the same source. It is of the same nature and quality. Our confidence in the faith we have been given increases as we exercise or operate in it. The way we utilized faith to receive our salvation is the same way we will use faith to receive everything else we receive from God. We already possess the adequate amount of faith necessary for us to see the manifestation of all the promises of God in our lives right now!

Our salvation is through faith. Every born-again believer has already operated in his or her faith's primary purpose. There is no greater exercise of faith than accepting Jesus Christ as Lord and Savior. If we are saved, we have already exercised our faith to its greatest potential possible. Everything else pales in its comparison! We would not have had the capacity or ability to get saved without having exercised the faith we have been given by God. The same faith we utilized to get saved, that enabled us to believe Jesus's death on the cross over 2000 years before our creation, in His burial and resurrection from the dead, is the same faith we must exercise in every area of our lives that we are desiring to experience manifestation.

2 Peter 1:3 AMPC. "For His divine power has bestowed upon us all things that [are requisite and suited] to life and godliness, through the [[a]full, personal] knowledge of Him Who called us by and to His own glory and excellence (virtue)"

Erroneously in the past, faith has been made out to be this elusive spiritual gift, only possessed by the deserving, select few. The rest of us have spent most of our spiritual lives respecting and admiring those who walked in great faith. Hoping to someday be spiritual or worthy enough to receive and experience the same kind of faith in our lives, we have either witnessed or heard of taking place in the lives of others.

As believers, we must grasp that God through His divine nature has already given us everything we need to navigate successfully through life. He has already given us everything requisite and suited for life and godliness including faith. We will only be able to walk in the measure of faith we have been given as we acquire and walk in the knowledge of our Father God's love for us.

Matthew 19:26 NIV "Jesus looked at them and said, "With man this is impossible, but with God all things are possible."

Everything is inclusive of all things and excludes nothing. Sit back, breathe in His presence and let that marinate for a few minutes. If we don't possess it, it means we haven't received it by faith. If I am a believer and I had the faith to believe there is a God in heaven, who sent His only Son named Jesus Christ to die for ME over 2000 years ago, and my acceptance of this makes me saved. Surely, today I have the capacity to believe I am healed of every disease or infirmity attacking my body. I can stand in the gap for my loved ones. I will see restoration in my family, walk-in financial wholeness and be a catalyst for change in my community. These are all minor in comparison to believing we are saved!

We were created by God to live faith-filled lives. Satan's strategy is to continuously get us to discount or underestimate the faithfulness of God to fulfill His Word to us and to cause us to doubt our ability to operate in faith. If we truly believe God to be a covenant keeper, we would not hesitate to trust Him completely. We demonstrate our trust in God by operating in faith. Knowing what the Word of God says is not enough. In order for the promises of God to be manifested in our lives we must mix our faith with the Word of God. Our faith is what activates or causes the promises of God to manifest in our individual lives.

Hebrews 4:1-4 KJV "Let us therefore fear, lest, a promise being left us of entering into his rest, any of you should seem to come short of it. For unto us was the gospel preached, as well as unto them:

but the word preached did not profit them, not being mixed with faith in them that heard it."

We are admonished throughout scripture to take heed or pay attention to the truth regarding God's promises concerning us. We are joint heirs with Christ and partners in faith of the Abrahamic Covenant. Being heirs of the promises of God alone does not make us automatic possessors. Many of us do not possess and are not walking in the blessings of God in our lives. We have come short of possessing our spiritual inheritance due to our lack of receiving and operating in the promises through faith We are aware of the blessings but don't walk in the blessings because of our unwillingness to demonstrate our trust in God by mixing our faith with the Word.

We were able to receive salvation through faith because we heard and believed the Good News or Gospel. Some of us heard about Jesus loving and dying for us from our parents or extended family, friends, attending church or through evangelistic tools or outreach. We may have heard the gospel from different avenues. However, we all have one thing in common. We each had to hear the gospel or good news before we were able to believe it. We heard and we attached faith to what we heard. We believed the gospel to be true. This is the foundation of salvation for the believer.

Romans 10:17 KJV "So then faith cometh by hearing, and hearing by the Word of God."

We cannot have faith for anything we have not heard. Many times, we must repeatedly hear something for us to believe it. Faith comes by hearing, and hearing by the Word of God. Each time we hear God's Word, we are being strengthened, developed and matured in our faith in the area we are hearing about. We received faith for salvation by hearing the Gospel of Grace. We acquired salvation by exercising our faith which made salvation accessible to us.

The same method of faith we utilized to obtain our salvation is the same method of faith we must utilize to obtain all the other promises of God in every area of our lives. The foundation of our salvation is built on Jesus's death, burial, and resurrection on the cross. The cross was the game-changer for every believer. Jesus Christ paid the penalty for all our sins. His death on the cross cleansed us from all past, present and future sin. NOW we can truly live the abundant life which He established for us.

Isaiah 53:5 AMPC "But He was wounded for our transgressions, He was bruised for our guilt and iniquities; the chastisement [needful to obtain] peace and well-being for us was upon Him, and with the stripes [that wounded] Him we are healed and made whole."

Salvation is just the first gift from God made accessible to believers through faith. Salvation through faith opened the door for us to receive our internal (emotional) and external (physical) healing and wholeness which were also purchased for us when Christ died on the cross. Jesus Christ's death on the cross was for our total peace and complete well-being. Our lives were redeemed on the cross and as a result, we were made whole; nothing missing or broken!

What if we feel we have enough faith to be saved but not enough faith to be healed? I believe this is the belief of most believers.   Faith comes ONLY by hearing and hearing ONLY by the Word of God. In this case, we need to read, study and listen to scriptures on healing until our faith for our healing is strengthened. God gave each of us the measure of faith. However, our faith is developed, strengthened and matured as we exercise our faith.

We exercise our faith by choosing to believe God's Word. The more we hear the Word of God, the more we will believe it. We become more intimately acquainted with Him through studying the bible and increasing our knowledge of Him. Most of us are at least willing to acknowledge we possess a small amount of faith. Jesus told the disciples that if they possessed faith the size of a mustard seed nothing would be impossible unto them.

Matthew 17:20 KJV "And Jesus said unto them, Because of your unbelief: for verily I say unto you, If ye have faith as a grain of mustard seed, ye shall say unto this mountain, Remove hence to yonder place; and it shall remove; and nothing shall be impossible unto you."

Jesus gave us a visual representation of the power of a little faith. If you have never seen an actual mustard seed, I recommend you go to the herbs and seasonings section, the next time you go to the grocery store, to see an actual mustard seed. This will help you to better understand the teachings on the power of faith. It is not the beginning size of the mustard seed that is impressive within itself. This seed would be despised if you didn't know it's potential. The mustard seed is very tiny, it is the smallest of seeds on earth (1 to 2 millimeters). The potential within the seed when planted and cultivated is truly amazing. The mustard seed can grow into an exceptional plant under ideal conditions that can reach up to 30 feet tall. A single mature mustard seed can grow into a plant/tree that houses birds. The mature plant can be used for cooking, medicinal purposes, dyeing of clothing, etc.

Jesus knew the example of the mustard seed would resonate greatly with His disciples. They were very familiar with its size. The disciples were Jesus's followers. They spent much time with Him day in and day out. He never put them down or tried to humiliate them. The focus of this passage of scripture is not the lack of faith possessed by the disciples. The focus of this passage is meant to be on the power encapsulated within a seemingly small seed that can accomplish great things once released.

We already have enough faith! We must stop minimizing the amount of faith we have and understand it is enough, just as it is, right where we are. We simply must exercise it. It is our faith mixed with the Word of God that produces manifestation every time. Jesus said we could speak to the mountains and if we doubted not, the mountains would have to obey us.

We understand that mountains are representative of situations in our lives that separate, block or hinder us from the blessings of God. Jesus is saying a little faith, spoken into our situation will cause the situation to move or change, just as speaking to the mountains in faith causes them to move out of our way, if we believe and doubt not in our hearts.

CHAPTER TWO FAITH NOTES

CHAPTER THREE

FAITH FUELED BY LOVE

1 John 4:10 NLT *"This is real love—not that we loved God, but that he loved us and sent his Son as a sacrifice to take away our sins"*

Faith works by love. Not by our loving God, but by the revelation of God's love for us. Our love towards God has been inconsistent, conditional and imperfect. It is flawed. God never intended for our faith to work based on our love for Him. He knew we could not bear the weight of that responsibility. God knew the only way it would work out right was for Him to be the source by which faith worked.

God is love personified. God's love for us is perfect. His love is long-suffering, unconditional and everlasting. God designed faith to work in our lives according to our revelation of how much He loves us. We can't grasp fully the depth of the Father's lavish love for us outside of a revelation of who God is. God is the embodiment of love through Jesus Christ.

John 3:16 AMPC "For God so greatly loved and dearly prized the world that He [even] gave up His only begotten ([a]unique) Son, so that whoever believes in (trusts in, clings to, relies on) Him shall not perish (come to destruction, be lost) but have eternal (everlasting) life."

It is God's love for us that fuels faith to work in our lives. It is His love for us which holds the key to opening the door for the manifestation of His promises in our lives. While we were yet sinners, God loved us so much, He sent Jesus to die for us. The Father's love for us reassures us of His faithfulness to us. The greatest benefit of being loved by God is His guarantee that He will take care of us. It serves as confirmation to us He will fulfill His every promise spoken to us through His Word.

We have had it mixed up or twisted for too long. We have failed to understand the key to all manifestation is the revelation of God's love for us. We simply must believe and rest in the truth that God loves us.

Faith comes alive and brings forth manifestation through the revelation of His love. We must grasp with the entirety of our being that God loves us. Our flawed focus has been on our loving Him and on our receiving manifestation as a result of our love for and faith in God. This belief put our receiving in limbo. It caused our manifestation to be determined by our love and faithfulness to God instead of His love and faithfulness to us.

Galatians 5:6 KJV "For in Jesus Christ neither circumcision availeth anything, nor uncircumcision; but faith which worketh by love."

In the past, we have believed and been more preoccupied with our level of love and commitment to God rather than focusing our attention on the magnitude of God's lavish, unconditional love for us. We always came up short. This was a satanic distraction, a ploy of the enemy. It was meant to keep us from developing an intimate relationship with the Father. He loves us with a perfect love. It is our awareness of His love for us that convinces and reassures us that He is dependable, and we can put our trust in Him.

We are the apple of our Father's eyes. He has already proven His love for us time and time again. He loves and prizes us above all things. We must know God loves us individually, so much that He would still give His life for the world even if we were the only one who would be saved. We must know that He is faithful to fulfill every promise given in scripture concerning us.

1 John 4:7-10 NIV "Dear friends, let us love one another, for love comes from God. Everyone who loves has been born of God and knows God. Whoever does not love does not know God, because God is love. This is how God showed his love among us: He sent his one and only Son into the world that we might live through him. This is love: not that we loved God, but that he loved us and sent his Son as an atoning sacrifice for our sins."

God is love. God does not possess love. He is the embodiment of love Himself. God in us causes us to be like Him. We love ourselves and others because He first loved us. Our love walk confirms we are His children. How do we get our faith to operate for us, on our behalf and the behalf of others? It begins with our knowledge and understanding of who God is. Faith will automatically begin to work in our lives as we engage the Father's love for us.

He is a good, good father. He loves us unconditionally. Our lives must be lived in the continual awareness of His love. We must know beyond a shadow of a doubt that He can be trusted. He cannot lie or be proven false. He does not disappoint or let anyone down who puts their faith in Him. He will never leave or forsake us.

Romans 8:35-39 KJV "Who shall separate us from the love of Christ? shall tribulation, or distress, or persecution, or famine, or nakedness, or peril or sword? As it is written, For thy sake we are killed all the day long; we are accounted as sheep for the slaughter. Nay, in all these things we are more than conquerors through him that loved us. For I am persuaded, that neither death, nor life, nor angels, nor principalities, nor powers, nor things present, nor things to come, Nor height, nor depth, nor any other creature, shall be able to separate us from the love of God, which is in Christ Jesus our Lord."

No one or nothing can separate us from God's love. His love is unconditional and eternal. God is faithful! Faith worketh as a result of our being confident in His love for us. The enemy of our faith desires for us to project our fear of being disappointed, rejected or abandoned onto God. He tells us God cannot be trusted because others we trusted let us down. Satan is a liar and the truth is not in Him. (St. John 8:44) He knows our faith can't work without our trust in God's love for us.

1 John 4:18 KJV "There is no fear in love; but perfect love casteth out fear: because fear hath torment. He that feareth is not made perfect in love."

The opposite of faith is not unbelief, it is fear. Kenneth Copeland made a profound statement, He said, "Fear tolerated is faith contaminated". This is absolutely true. This means our faith loses its ability to work when fear is present. Faith is rendered inoperable by our fear of failure. It is impossible to be in fear and faith at the same time. God is love. He does not give us fear. Fear destroys faith. There is no fear in God at all.

1 John 4:18 KJV "There is no fear in love; but perfect love casteth out fear: because fear hath torment. He that feareth is not make perfect in love."

Faith operates by love. Faith says because I am loved by God, everything will work out for my good. Fear says it will hurt me, and I will somehow lose. Love brings freedom and liberty. Fear brings torment and bondage. Fear will keep us from flying in an airplane because we are afraid it may crash. Fear will keep us from taking a cruise because we are afraid the ship might sink, and we may drown. We won't step out in faith on God's Word because you are afraid it will break down underneath you. Fear torments its possessor. Perfect love takes hold of fear and casts it out.

2 Timothy 1:7-9 AMPC "For God did not give us a spirit of timidity (of cowardice, of craven and cringing and fawning fear), but [He has given us a

spirit] of power and of love and of calm and well-balanced mind and discipline and self-control"

God does not want us to walk through life afraid. Faith in God's love keeps us from living fear-filled lives. His love reassures us that we don't have to worry about losing our life prematurely. Whenever fear tries to invade our lives, we must remind ourselves that fear is not of God. Therefore, fear does not have a legal right to remain in our lives as sons and daughters of God. God loves us! Our faith in God's ability to keep us safe should be just as powerful when we are on a plane 40,000 feet in the air, as it is when we are on the ground. God is just as much with us, when we are in a ship on the ocean, as He is when we are at home sitting in front of the television. Fear will flee from us as we gain a revelation of God's unfailing love for us. God has no limitations. He is with us everywhere we go.

Matthew 28:20 KJV "Teaching them to observe all things whatsoever I have commanded you: and, lo, I am with you always, even unto the end of the world. Amen."

God has given us power, love and a sound mind. We received these when we received salvation. We have the spiritual authority to reject or refuse to accept anything that is not from God. Knowing we are loved should govern your behavior or actions as well as our emotional well-being. The revelation of God's love for us should decrease our feelings of anxiety and depression. Hope springs from love and love keeps us from shame. Remember, it is the revelation of God's love for us that fuels our faith.

Romans 5:5 KIV "And hope does not put us to shame, because God's love has been poured out into our hearts through the Holy Spirit, who has been given to us."

CHAPTER THREE FAITH NOTES

CHAPTER FOUR

FAITH IN GOD'S FAITHFULNESS

1 Corinthians 1:9 KJV "God is faithful, by whom ye were called unto the fellowship of his Son Jesus Christ our Lord."

We must stop projecting our distrust with man onto a faithful God. Many of us have been disappointed by those who were in a position of authority or significance in our lives. We may have been hurt by our parent(s), guardian, caregiver or spouse. In our hearts and minds, they failed us. Regardless of whether it was intentional or not. In our eyes, they did not love us unconditionally, provide for us or protect us like we expected them to. These experiences resulted in many of us having major trust issues. We may now find it extremely difficult to truly trust any man. Well, God is not a man!

We do God a disservice when we try to relegate Him to the status of a mere human being. We must stop blaming God for their shortcomings. God can not lie, and He does not change His mind about what He has spoken concerning us. He has never let anyone down who has put their trust in Him. Again, God is not man. Faithfulness is not just a characteristic of God. Faithful is who God is. The failings and shortcomings of others have nothing to do with God.

Numbers 23:19 KJV "God is not a man, that he should lie; neither the son of man, that he should repent: hath he said, and shall he not do it? or hath he spoken, and shall he not make it good?"

Faith in God's faithfulness requires we let go of all the past misconceptions we have had about God ever letting us down. Believing in God's faithfulness is an act of faith. We must exercise faith in the faithfulness of God to walk in the manifestation of His promises. God is trustworthy and forever true to His Word. Whatever God says He will do, He will do.

He will make it good. Once we have a revelation of God's faithfulness to His Word nothing will be impossible unto us.

Romans 3:3-4 KJV "For what if some did not believe? shall their unbelief make the faith of God without effect? God forbid: yea, let God be true, but every man a liar; as it is written, That thou mightest be justified in thy sayings, and mightest overcome when thou art judged."

God remains forever faithful to His Word. What if we are faithless or if everyone does not believe God will fulfill His promises in our lives? Does that change His faithfulness to us? Absolutely NOT! God does not require anyone to cosign or believe what He has declared concerning our lives. There are no prerequisites for Him to fulfill His promises to us but our faith in Him. God signs His own checks. He does not need a cosigner. *Hebrews 12:2a KJV "Looking unto Jesus the author and finisher of our faith".* The manifestation of the promises of God in our lives is solely dependent on our believing God.

1 Thessalonians 5:24 KJV "Faithful is he that calleth you, who also will do it."

Anyone who says God needs them to agree with Him before He fulfills His Word to us is mistaken or a liar. We should be encouraged and strengthened in our faith knowing our faithlessness or other people's lack of belief do not affect God's faithfulness to us. Our manifestation is only about us standing on God's Word and knowing He is faithful to fulfill it.

II Corinthians 1:20 KJV "For all the promises of God in him are yea, and in him Amen, unto the glory of God by us ".

God's faithfulness to us is a representation of His character and integrity. God's faithfulness to us does not have an expiration date. His promises are just as reliable today as they were when He made them. God keeps covenant or agreement with His children for a thousand generations. His covenant is everlasting. God is faithful to keep every promise to us. His response or answer to us concerning His words are always yes and amen.

Deuteronomy 7:9 KJV "Know therefore that the Lord thy God, he is God, the faithful God, which keepeth covenant and mercy with them that love him and keep his commandments to a thousand generations;"

God is faithful even when it looks as though He isn't. Many times, we allow the delay to cause us to question the faithfulness of God. We ask why is it taking so long? We feel like if God was going to do it, it would have happened by now. I surmise that the delay can be for our good. The delay is simply an opportunity for us to exercise our faith in God's faithfulness.

2 Thessalonians 3:3 KJV "But the Lord is faithful, who shall stablish you, and keep you from evil "

If we truly believe God is faithful the delay will not impact us negatively. The delay will help to develop us by manifesting the thoughts of our mind and the deep contents of hearts to us. Delay will show us and others where we really are concerning our trust in God's faithfulness to us.

2 Timothy 2:13 AMPC "If we are faithless [do not believe and are untrue to Him], He remains true (faithful to His Word and His righteous character), for He cannot deny Himself."

Everyone can trust God for a little while. What happens to us when it looks like our faith isn't working? If we start doubting and start accusing God, this demonstrates we do not totally trust Him. Our wavering in faith does not cause God to become unfaithful to us. He remains faithful to His Word. If we find that we are not in faith, that somewhere along the road we got off track, instead of giving up altogether, all we need to do is refocus on the Word and get back in faith.

What we are saying during the delay reveals our trust in God's faithfulness. Faith in God's faithfulness is demonstrated by our remaining steadfast in our belief in God in the meantime, while we are waiting for manifestation. We must consistently and continually say what God has said about our situation even when it appears in the natural that things are getting worse. Faith in God is heard through the confession of our faith. It is impossible to be in faith and the words preceding out of our mouths be filled with doubt and unbelief. From the abundance of the heart the mouth speaks. (St. Luke 6:45). What we believe will come out of our mouth during times of stress or delay. Our words reflect our faith in God's faithfulness.

Hebrews 10:23 KJV "Let us hold fast the profession of our faith without wavering; (for he is faithful that promised;"

CHAPTER FOUR FAITH NOTES

CHAPTER FIVE

IT'S A FAITH FIGHT!

Hebrews 10:35-36 AMPC "Do not, therefore, fling away your fearless confidence, for it carries a great and glorious compensation of reward. For you have need of steadfast patience and endurance, so that you may perform and fully accomplish the will of God, and thus receive and [a]carry away [and enjoy to the full] what is promised."

In a faith fight, it does not matter what it looks or feels like, if we are obeying God, we are winning! Faith is not a feeling. Faith is knowing God is faithful to fulfill His Word. Webster's defines fight as to contend in battle. The battleground for every faith fight is always in the mind. We are in a faith fight or standing in faith when we are defending or refusing to relinquish our *"assurance (the confirmation, the title deed) of the things [we] hope for, being the proof of things [we] do not see and the conviction of their reality [faith perceiving as real fact what is not revealed to the senses]" according to Hebrews 11:1 AMPC.* We must constantly refuse to relinquish our faith. Our faith is the most valuable asset we will ever possess during a faith fight. It is our responsibility to fight to keep it. A faith fight is not a stroll in the park. It is being engaged in spiritual battle. It is our contending for the faith. When it looks as though we are losing, faith in God's faithfulness to fulfill His promises to us, is the only way we can stand. We must not rely on others to keep us encouraged. We must learn to encourage ourselves in the Lord and hold on tight to our confession of faith.

St. John 16:33 AMPC "I have told you these things, so that in Me you may have [perfect] peace and confidence. In the world you have tribulation and trials and distress and frustration; but be of good cheer [take courage; be confident, certain, undaunted]! For I have overcome the world. [I have deprived it of power to harm you and have it for you.]

Don't throw it away in frustration or during seasons of doubt or delay. We must learn to take care of ourselves and parameter our minds during a faith fight. There are simple things we can do in the natural to decrease our levels of frustration during a faith fight. H.A.L.T is a synonym easy to remember. It would help our emotional disposition to remain calmer and more stable if we would not allow ourselves to get extremely Hungry, Angry, Lonely or Tired. Remembering this, will help to decrease our irritability and frustration. We should always take care of ourselves physically but especially during a faith fight. It's easier to fight spiritually when we are not battling physical challenges at the same time.

1 Corinthians 6:19 KJV "What? Know ye not that your body is the temple of the Holy Ghost which is in you, which he have of God, and ye are not your own?"

The way we feel while in a faith fight cannot be trusted. Our feelings have proven to be unreliable and deceptive witnesses in the past. It is foolish to allow feelings to direct our actions. Feelings originate from the carnal or soulish realm. We all have experienced seasons in our spiritual lives when we felt our faith was not working for us. It appeared we were believing in vain. We may have felt we were losing everything, and nothing was working out the way we planned. During these seasons it may appear like what we are seeing is the opposite of what we are believing for and in the natural, it may even appear our situation has worsened.

St. Luke 1:37 NIV "For no word from God will ever fail."

We contend for the faith by standing flat-footed on the Word of God and refusing to budge regardless of how things look or how we feel. It would not be a fight if there was no opposition or opponent to our position of faith. Our opponent is always the devil. Satan attacks us in our minds because he knows the battle is won or lost based on our thought life. During a faith fight, it's impossible to have everything go our way.

We must be willing to relinquish control of our lives to God and accept that things most likely will not go exactly as we have imagined or planned. Frustration is inevitable. Delay is one of the most used strategies of Satan.

We all will get extremely tired sometimes while believing God and waiting on the manifestation of His promises. Don't throw in the towel. Remind yourself that it's a fixed fight. We win every time if we stay in faith and don't quit. We are not trying to obtain the victory. God gave us the victory. We are winning right now. Correction: We have already won!

1 Corinthians 15:57 NIV "But thanks be to God! He gives us the victory through our Lord Jesus Christ."

Scripture tells us to fight the good fight of faith, to aim at and pursue righteousness. To walk in faith, love, steadfastness (patience) and gentleness of heart. To lay hold of eternal life. The reward or compensation for the victor is the manifestation of God's promises. We must be determined to stand indefinitely. How long do we wait patiently for the promises of God in our lives? Until they manifest!

1 Timothy 6:11-12 AMPC "But as for you, O man of God, flee from all these things; aim at and pursue righteousness (right standing with God and true goodness), godliness (which is the loving fear of God and being Christlike), faith, love, steadfastness (patience), and gentleness of heart. Fight the good fight of the faith; lay hold of the eternal life to which you were summoned and [for which] you confessed the good confession [of faith] before many witnesses."

We want the manifestation of what we are believing for to occur immediately, however in a faith fight, we cannot allow our impatience to get the best of us. In order to receive and enjoy what God has promised us we must employ our patience. We cannot allow our frustration to cause us to throw away our confidence in the Word of God. Our compensation (manifestation) is attached to our faith. No faith, no manifestation.

1 Peter 5:7-8 AMPC "Casting the [a]whole of your care [all your anxieties, all your worries, all your concerns, [b]once and for all] on Him, for He cares for you affectionately and cares about you [c]watchfully. Be well balanced (temperate, sober of mind), be vigilant and cautious at all times; for that enemy of yours, the devil, roams around like a lion roaring [[d]in fierce hunger], seeking someone to seize upon and devour."

God does not want us full of anxiety and worry while we are standing on the Word. He's a good, good Father. He cares affectionately and watchfully for us. We must possess the right mindset while we are in a faith fight. Meditating on and studying the Word of God is mandatory for us if we plan on walking in peace while we await manifestation. The only way to avoid casting or flinging away our confidence during extremely difficult times is to instead cast all our anxieties, worries and concerns on Him. We must be well balanced, temperate and sober of mind. Cautious always. Why? Satan is going about as a roaring lion seeking to seize upon and devour our faith. Satan is a toothless bully. He is a big talker. He makes a lot of noise. He attacks our thinking and He tricks us into relinquishing the victory that Christ has already won for us. He does this because he fears our faith. He knows our faith guarantees us manifestation every time.

1 Corinthians 15:57-58 AMPC "But thanks be to God, Who gives us the victory [making us conquerors] through our Lord Jesus Christ. Therefore, my beloved brethren, be firm (steadfast), immovable, always abounding in the work of the Lord [always being superior, excelling, doing more than enough in the service of the Lord], knowing and being continually aware that your labor in the Lord is not futile [it is never wasted or to no purpose]."

God gives us the victory every time. He has already made us more than conquerors through our Lord and Savior Jesus Christ. It's a fixed fight! We cannot lose. We are not trying to become victorious. We are thanking God that we are already victorious in Him. All we must do is determine in our minds and spirit that we are going to stand firm, immovable on God's Word continuously. We assume the position of conqueror that He has already given to us. We stand through our studying, believing and confessing His Word. God and the

Word are one. As we study the Word of God, we become one with it and become more like God.

The will of God is the Word of God. Studying the Bible acquaints us with God's integrity and character. It intimately reveals to us His love (heart) and intentions (mind) towards us. Studying God's Word connects us to His mind, nature, and way of doing things. Faith cometh by hearing. The more we study God's Word, the more we will believe it. Our mouths confess what we believe. We must strive to remain steadfast in our worship and obedient service to God during our faith fight. We should not decrease in our faithfulness. We are superior, we excel and do more than what is required of us.

Ephesians 6:12 KJV "For we wrestle not against flesh and blood, but against principalities, against powers, against the rulers of the darkness of this world, against spiritual wickedness in high places."

We are not fighting or wrestling against another human being. Our opponent is not flesh and blood. Our enemy is Satan. He does not fight fair. His assignment is to steal, kill and destroy. The faith fight is a spiritual battle and it can only be fought and won in the spirit. It is our responsibility to be properly equipped when we enter a spiritual battle.

2 Corinthians 10:4-5 AMPC "For the weapons of our warfare are not physical [weapons of flesh and blood], but they are mighty before God for the overthrow and destruction of strongholds, [Inasmuch as we] refute arguments and theories and reasonings and every proud and lofty thing that sets itself up against the [true] knowledge of God; and we lead every thought and purpose away captive into the obedience of Christ (the Messiah, the Anointed One),"

It is impossible to fight a spiritual battle with physical weapons. We must utilize spiritual weapons if we desire to be successful. We can only fight this battle with the Word of God. The target of the attack (family, health, finances) may change but the weapons of our warfare and the battleground will always be the same. The weapons are spiritual, and the battleground will always be our mind. God has created and given us powerful weapons, to use in our spiritual battles, however; they are useless if we don't use them. They were designed for the overthrow and destruction of strongholds, houses of thought or fortified ways of thinking. When we are in a faith fight, we must obtain scriptures to stand on regarding whatever area we are fighting for.

We are not fighting to obtain or get anything from God. We are fighting to maintain or keep the thief from stealing what we already possess. We are standing on the Word and refusing to allow him to steal our victory from us. For example, if we are being attacked in our health, we stand on healing scriptures such as *Isaiah 53:5 KJV "But he was wounded for our transgressions, he was bruised for our iniquities: the chastisement of our peace was upon him; and with his stripes we are healed"* and *Psalms 103:3 NIV "who forgives all your sins and heals all diseases, ".* If we are being attacked in our finances, we can stand on *Philippians 4:19 KJV* *"But my God shall supply all your need according to his riches in glory by Christ Jesus."*

I am an honorably discharged veteran. When I joined the military, they issued me both a weapon and a uniform. Although they were issued to me, I had to receive training to learn to use my weapon (M-16 Assault Rifle) and instructions on how to correctly wear my battle gear. The same is true for us as children of God. He has issued us not only weapons to fight with but armor to defend ourselves. It is our responsibility to become students of God's Word and to learn how to put on our spiritual armor.

God has done everything within His power to guarantee our victory in life. He gave us the victory and the ability to keep what He has given us. The greatest piece of armor that we have been given is the shield of faith. Faith is referred to as a shield for several reasons. A shield is both a defensive and offensive weapon. A shield can be used as a covering, for protection, to deflect attacks and to quench the fiery darts of the wicked one in whatever area we utilize it.

Our faith guarantees us the manifestation of the promises of God in our lives if we don't quit. Faith is required to win the battle and walk in victory. Faith encompasses our trust in God. Faith demonstrates our understanding of God's love for us. Faith affords us patience and perseverance. All things are possible to us when we believe. Faith does not need evidence to substantiate it and delay does not invalidate it. Faith sustains itself. Faith cannot be minimized. How long do we wait? How long do we remain in our faith fight? Until our victory manifest!

Ephesians 6:11-18 KJV "Put on the whole armour of God, that ye may be able to stand against the wiles of the devil. For we wrestle not against flesh and blood, but against principalities, against powers, against the rulers of the darkness of this world, against spiritual wickedness in high places. Wherefore take unto you the whole armour of God, that ye may be able to withstand in the evil day, and having done all, to stand. Stand therefore, having your loins girt about with truth, and having on the breastplate of righteousness; And your feet shod with the preparation of the gospel of peace; Above all, taking the shield of faith, wherewith ye shall be able to quench all the fiery darts of the wicked. And take the helmet of salvation, and the sword of the Spirit, which is the word of God: for all saints;"

CHAPTER FIVE FAITH NOTES

_____

_____

_____

_____

_____

_____

_____

_____

_____

_____

_____

_____

_____

_____

CHAPTER SIX

FAITHING IT!

2 Corinthians 5:7 KJV "For we walk by faith, not by sight"

We are spirits, we possess souls and we occupy bodies. Although spirits, we are journeying through life in fleshly earth suits. Most of our daily lives are guided or totally influenced by our natural perceptions. We rely on what we see, feel, smell and touch to navigate successfully through our natural lives. We rightfully depend on our natural senses for everything except for our spirituality. Natural senses are useless when it comes to following God.

We must shift gears completely when it comes to our faith walk. We must abandon our natural senses and depend solely on what the Word of God tells us regarding our lives. As believers, we must be led by our spirit man which is always in agreement with the Word of God.

Our spiritual journey was designed by God to totally be a walk of faith. Another name or term used by some believers for walking by faith is *Faithing It.* What exactly do we mean when we say we are *Faithing It?* What does *Faithing It* look like in the believer's life during times of struggle? Is this the same thing as faking it? No, it is not! There is no such thing as faking while in faith. For believers, the Word of God carries final authority in our lives and His Word is more real to us than what we see.

Hebrews 11:6 KJV "But without faith it is impossible to please him: for he that cometh to God must believe that he is, and that he is a rewarder of them that diligently seek him."

The difference between *Faithing It* and faking is when we are faking, we are pretending to be something that we are not, or that our situation is different than it really is. Faking is pretending. It is living a lie. It's saying something that we do not believe to be true. For the believer what may be factual about our situation yet may not be our truth. Our truth is always established by the Word of God.

Faithing It is self-identifying, seeing ourselves as the Word of God says we are, and not as our present reality is depicting or manifesting our lives as being. *Faithing It* is believing what the Word of God says despite what we may be experiencing. *Faithing It* is allowing God's Word to be more real to us than what we are presently experiencing. *Faithing It* is living according to the dictates of the spirit and not according to our flesh or the seen realm.

Romans 4:17 AMP "As it is written, I have made you the father of many nations. [He was appointed our father] in the sight of God in Whom he believed, Who gives life to the dead and speaks of the nonexistent things that [He has foretold and promised] as if they [already] existed."

Faithing It is continuing to call those things that be not as though they are. It is speaking of the non-existent things as though they exist. *Faithing It* is not denying that a certain situation or circumstance exist in the natural realm. *Faithing It* is denying that it has a right to remain in or govern our lives. We believe if what we are dealing with is not a part of our spiritual inheritance that we do not have to accept it as our permanent reality according to the Word of God.

Faithing It is choosing to live day by day trusting in the Word of God concerning every area of our lives regardless of what it looks like in the natural realm. This does NOT mean that we are not going to have faith fights along the way. *Faithing It* is not being in denial. Yes, at times as believers we will be challenged in our bodies. Some of us may have been diagnosed with a chronic or terminal illness or disease. Others may be experiencing pain or discomfort in their bodies. This does not mean we don't have faith. Faith that is seen is not faith. If we believe we are healed, we are healed. We don't have to feel healed to be healed. Faithing It says we are healed NOW, awaiting the full manifestation of our complete healing. We choose to identify with the Word of God instead of with what we are experiencing in our bodies.

Psalms 30:2 KJV "O Lord My God, I cried unto thee and thou has healed me."

Faithing It does NOT mean we do not take medications or go to the doctor while awaiting manifestation. I suggest you DO go to a Christian doctor and follow His godly advice. Surgery and medication are good things if they improve the quality of our lives. *Faithing It* means regardless of what the doctor says we yet believe the Word of God. The Word of God ALWAYS has final authority in our lives. *Faithing It* is acknowledging sickness may be attacking our bodies; however, we continue to believe we are NOT sick. We do not take ownership of or self-identify with sickness. Faithing It is self-identifying with or seeing ourselves as being healed according to God's Word.

Isaiah 53:5 KJV "But he was wounded for our transgressions, he was bruised for our iniquities: the chastisement of our peace was upon him; and with his stripes we are healed"

What does *Faithing It* look like in the believer's life during a major faith fight? Sometimes while in a major faith fight, we can remain strong in faith. It appears we go from believing to receiving manifestation without delay. However, there are often times during intense faith fights when it looks like we are struggling greatly to stay in faith. We may even experience periods of doubting or questioning if our faith is working at all. It can feel like we are literally fighting for our lives. It may feel as if we are about to lose our minds. We may be experiencing a prolonged satanic attack in our minds that have left us battling doubt, fear, anxiety, depression, rejection, isolation, unforgiveness, etc. During an intense faith fight, we need to immerse ourselves in the Word of God continuously.

Isaiah 26:3 AMPC "You will guard him and keep him in perfect and constant peace who mind [both its inclination and its character] is stayed on You, because he commits himself to You, leans on You, and hopes confidently in You."

Don't give up. Regardless of how difficult things may be. Don't quit. It's a fixed fight. We win! Sometimes it is hard to not identify with what is attacking us. We may be struggling with not receiving or accepting into our spirit man what is attacking us in our physical body. We must refuse to take ownership of the doctor's negative diagnosis, symptoms of pain and discomfort that may be trying to lure us into taking our focus off the Word of God.

2 Corinthians 4:17 AMPC "For our slight momentary affliction (this slight distress of the passing hour) is ever more and more abundantly preparing and producing and achieving for us an everlasting weight of glory [beyond all measure, excessively surpassing all comparisons and all calculations, vast and transcendent glory and blessedness never to cease!]

Faithing It does not mean we won't have periods of doubting. We are human and sometimes our emotions will try to overwhelm us spiritually. Therefore, we cannot rely on our feelings. Sometimes it may look and feel as though we are losing. It may appear like our faith is not producing what we are believing for. We may be going through the most difficult season of our lives. We may be convinced no one understands what we are experiencing, and we may feel abandoned.

Romans 8:24-26 KJV "For we are saved by hope: but hope that is seen is not hope: for what a man seeth, why doth he yet hopes for? But if we hope for that we see not, then do we with patience wait for it. Likewise the Spirit also helpeth our infirmities: for we know not what we should pray for as we ought: but the Spirit itself maketh intercession for us with groanings which cannot be uttered."

God knew there would be very trying times in our lives. God gave us the Holy Spirit to help us. The Holy Spirit makes intercession for us during difficult times especially when it looks and feels like we are losing. It may even appear our situation is getting worse instead of better. Our bank account may be in the negative or red. We may have had homes or cars repossessed or foreclosed on. Our situation may say that we are destitute.

We don't have to identify with the lack that may presently exist in our lives. God created us to not be comfortable with debt or lack. It should not be where we see ourselves permanently. This temporal situation is NOT our permanent destination or final outcome. We will not self-identify with the lack of financial resources we may be presently experiencing. We refuse to take ownership of poverty or lack because this is not our inheritance.

We are not faking. We truly believe the attack against our health and finances is temporal. We align our words and actions with what God has spoken about our health and finances. We declare God's Word regarding them. I am the lender and not the borrower, I am above only and not beneath.

Philippians 4:19 AMPC "But my God will liberally supply (fill to the full) your every need according to His riches in glory by Christ Jesus."

Faithing It is more than just saying the right things or trying to sound spiritual. It is not 'name it, claim it' foolishness. Faith always carries with it corresponding action. Faith without works is nonexistent or dead. While *Faithing It* we still must take care of our health. We eat healthy and exercise. We respect our temples. *Faithing It* during financial difficulties requires that we be good financial stewards. We are faithful tithers. We don't rob God. We manage our money wisely. We don't live above our means. Living by faith is not a new phenomenon. Believers have been doing it since before Christ. They are witnesses to us to remain in faith and Keep *Faithing It.*

Hebrews 12:1-2 KJV "Wherefore seeing we also are compassed about with so great a cloud of witnesses, let us lay aside every weight, and the sin which doth so easily beset us, and let us run with patience the race that is set before us, Looking unto Jesus the author and finisher of our faith; who for the joy that was set before him endured the cross, despising the shame, and is set down at the right hand of the throne of God.

HEBREW CHAPTER 11 ~ HEROES OF FAITH

NOAH

Hebrews 11:7 KJV "By faith Noah, being warned of God of things not seen as yet, moved with fear, prepared an ark to the saving of his house; by which he condemned the world, and became heir of the righteousness which is by faith."

ABRAHAM

Hebrews 11:8-10 KJV "By faith Abraham, when he was called to go out into a place which he should after receive for an inheritance, obeyed; and he went out, not knowing whither he went. By faith he sojourned in the land of promise, as in a strange country, dwelling in tabernacles with Isaac and Jacob, the heirs with him of the same promise: For he looked for a city which hath foundations, whose builder and maker is God."

Hebrews 11:17-19 "By faith Abraham, when he was tried, offered up Isaac: and he that had received the promises offered up his only begotten son, 18 Of whom it was said, That in Isaac shall thy seed be called: 19 Accounting that God was able to raise him up, even from the dead; from whence also he received him in a figure."

SARA

Hebrews 11:11 KJV "Through faith also Sara herself received strength to conceive seed, and was delivered of a child when she was past age, because she judged him faithful who had promised. Therefore sprang there even of one, and him as good as dead, so many as the stars of the sky in multitude, and as the sand which is by the sea shore innumerable."

ISAAC

Hebrews 11:20 KJV "By faith Isaac blessed Jacob and Esau concerning things to come."

JACOB

Hebrews 11:21 KJV "By faith Jacob, when he was a dying, blessed both the sons of

Joseph; and worshipped, leaning upon the top of his staff. "

JOSEPH

Hebrews 11:22 KJV "By faith Joseph, when he died, made mention of the departing of the children of Israel; and gave commandment concerning his bones."

MOSES

Hebrews 11:23-29 KJV "By faith Moses, when he was born, was hid three months of his parents, because they saw he was a proper child; and they were not afraid of the king's commandment. By faith Moses, when he was come to years, refused to be called the son of Pharaoh's daughter; Choosing rather to suffer affliction with the people of God, than to enjoy the pleasures of sin for a season; Esteeming the reproach of Christ greater riches than the treasures in Egypt: for he had respect unto the recompence of the reward. By faith he forsook Egypt, not fearing the wrath of the king: for he endured, as seeing him who is invisible. Through faith he kept the passover, and the sprinkling of blood, lest he that destroyed the firstborn should touch them. By faith they passed through the Red sea as by dry

land: which the Egyptians assaying to do were drowned."

CHAPTER SIX FAITH NOTES

CHAPTER *SEVEN*

NOW, FAITH IS!

Hebrews 11:1 AMPC "Now faith is the assurance (the confirmation, the title deed) of the things [we] hope for, being the proof of things [we] do not see and the conviction of their reality [faith perceiving as real fact what is not revealed to the senses].

Scripture does not say faith was or faith shall be, it states "Now, faith is". Faith is a present tense word or noun. Faith is a right-now spiritual substance. Faith is a present time assurance, confirmation and title deed of the things we are hoping for. Our faith is evidence we presently possess or have spiritual ownership of what is not yet visible or tangible in the natural realm. Our faith substantiates the existence of what we know already exists in the spirit before it manifests. It is our proof of its reality, causing us to perceive as fact what has not yet been manifested to our natural senses.

Faith is not things or stuff. Faith is not restored relationships, good health, or financial prosperity. We cannot behold faith as we do a natural object. It is not the house, car, or job. Faith is the creative substance that brings into manifestation the things we are believing for. Faith cannot be seen or touched. If we can see it, it is not faith. Faith allows us to take legal custody in the spiritual realm of what we do not yet possess in the natural realm.

Romans 8:24-25 KJV "For we are saved by hope: but hope that is seen is not hope: for what a man seeth, why doth he yet hope for? But if we hope for that we see not, then do we with patience wait for it."

THE PROCESS OF FAITH

STEP ONE ~ HEARING

Romans 10:17 KJV "So then faith cometh by hearing, and hearing by the word of God."

It does matter what we are hearing. The amount of faith we have in the Word of God, and the level of faith we operate in daily, is directly proportional to the amount of teaching on faith we have heard. Listening to faith teachings and hearing testimonies about other's faith will encourage and motivate us in our own walk of faith. Faith comes to us by hearing and rehearing of the Word of God ONLY.

We are strengthened in our faith in the area we are hearing or studying. If we are struggling in our bodies, we need to hear God's word or scriptures regarding healings. If we are struggling in our marriages, we need scriptures on the covenant of marriage. If we are struggling in our finances, we need to hear scriptures about God being our source. While in faith, we need to hear specific scripture pertaining to exactly what we are dealing with. Hearing is the beginning or entrance of knowledge. *"Faith begins where the will of God is known"* F.F. Bosworth.

We will never know anything that we have not heard. Hearing is our sole responsibility. We can't blame the preacher or teacher for what we don't know. It's our responsibility to study our bible for ourselves. We need to continually hear the Word of God. Faith does not come by what we heard yesterday or by what we may hear tomorrow. Faith comes by what we are presently hearing. It amazes me how we will spend money without thinking on material things that do not benefit us spiritually but will hesitate to spend $15 on a faith C.D. or book that will change our lives forever. We must be willing to invest in our spiritual development.

2 Timothy 2:15 KJV "Study to shew thyself approved unto God, a workman that needed not to be ashamed, rightly dividing the word of truth.

Possessing strong faith does not happen by accident. Strong faith is developed on purpose. It is the result of intentionally hearing and rehearing the Word of God. Each day life challenges us as believers to either walk by sight or by faith.

Challenges and distractions are never going to leave us. We all are allotted the same 24-hours in a day. We must value the Word of God enough to set aside or make time for our spiritual development.

Hosea 4:6a KJV "My people are destroyed for lack of knowledge"

STEP TWO ~ BELIEVING

Mark 11:24 KJV "Therefore I say unto you, What things soever ye desire, when ye pray, believe that ye receive them, and ye shall have them."

Believing springs from hearing. It's impossible to believe what we have not heard. Each time we hear the Word of God we make a choice to believe it by faith or to reject it. We can't fake believing. The choice is always ours. Believing carries with it corresponding actions. Most believers believe in the power of God to perform miracles, yet we don't know for sure He will do it for us.

There is a big difference between believing God is able or can do something, to believing God will or has already completed it specifically for us. What we believe carries us from being spectators or witnesses of faith operating in the lives of others to participators of faith in action in our own lives.

Hebrews 11:6 "But without faith it is impossible to please him: for he that cometh to God must believe that he is, and that he is a rewarder of them that diligently seek him."

We must believe that God is more than JUST ABLE to heal us. We must believe we are already healed according to *Isaiah 53:5 KJV "But he was wounded for our transgressions, he was bruised for our iniquities: the chastisement of our peace was upon him; and with his stripes we are healed."* A belief is not a feeling. When in a faith fight our outcome is dependent on our beliefs not our feelings. They are two separate things. Feelings come from our soul (mind, will and emotions). They are not dependable. Faith is an operation of our spirit man. We must believe we are already healed for our healing to manifest.

We must also stop asking for provisions (food, clothing, and shelter) and start thanking Him in advance for supplying all our needs. We must grasp in our hearts and believe regardless of what it looks like, that we do not have any unmet needs according to *Philippians 4:19 "But my God shall supply all your need according to his riches in glory by Christ Jesus."*

STEP THREE ~ SPEAKING

Mark 11:22-23 KJV "And Jesus answering saith unto them, Have faith in God. For verily I say unto you, That whosoever shall say unto this mountain, Be thou removed, and be thou cast into the sea; and shall not doubt in his heart, but shall believe that those things which he saith shall come to pass; he shall have whatsoever he saith."

Faith manifests its presence through our speech. It does matter what we are saying. The words that come out of our mouths reflect our beliefs. Anytime that we want to know what someone believes all we have to do is listen to them talk. Our beliefs are a result of what we have been consistently hearing. Our words must agree with God's Word in order for us to have the Godkind of results. God and His Word are one. When we speak the Word, we release God into the atmosphere.

We cannot separate the words we speak from what we believe. The words we are presently speaking are the verbal expression of our present beliefs. This means it is impossible to be in faith and not speak faith-filled words. Faith manifests itself spiritually through our words prior to its manifestation in the natural realm.

Our faith-filled words identify us as being one with the Word of God or as our being separate. God is holy because He is one with His Word. We become one with God through our believing and speaking His words. Each time we speak and release faith-filled words, we are reconstructing or framing our lives. Through the Word of God, we can create our world, the same way God created the universe.

In the natural we may use a Global Positioning System (G.P.S) to guide us to a predetermined destination we may not be familiar with. We must know where we are going in order to have information to input into the G.P.S. We don't have to know how to get there. Our words set the course of our lives. Faith cannot bring into manifestation what we are believing for until we speak it. The G.P.S will not give us directions until we input where we want to go. When we speak, we are spiritually programming in inputting our destiny into the atmosphere the same way we input our destination into the G.P.S.

We are creative beings, when we speak, we are setting the course of our lives. We are framing our world by the words of our mouth. What if we have been making negative confessions, saying the wrong thing or have gotten completely off course? We don't just stop traveling midway our journey. We can't undo the past or take back words spoken. We stop right where we are, repent and immediately start speaking the Word of God concerning every area of our lives. We recalculate or renew our commitment of walking by faith. It does matter what you are speaking. The method believers use to set or establish what we desire to see manifested in our lives is always determined by what we are saying.

Hebrews 11:3 KJV "Through faith we understand that the worlds were framed by the word of God, so that things which are seen were not made of things which do appear."

Our faith upholds us. It will not break down beneath us. It stabilizes our feet. Faith is our guarantee that manifestation is absolute. When we possess faith, it does not matter to us who understands or approves of our stance. We are persuaded and we believe the Word of God. Faith is a creative force within each of us that increases or decreases based on our trust in the Word of God.

However, when we are in faith, we are not currently experiencing or seeing manifestation. Faith and manifestation or works are completely different things. Faith is the unseen substance we use to bring into existence the manifestation. We must continually speak it before it manifests. After it manifests, there will be no need to speak about it because it will be visible for everyone to see. If we will remain in faith, the outward manifestation is guaranteed. More importantly, even before we see the full manifestation of what we are believing for, we along with others will see grace and patience being manifested in our daily lives while we are waiting.

2 Corinthians 4:13 "We having the same spirit of faith, according as it is written, I believed, and therefore have I spoken; we also believe, and therefore speak;"

A byproduct of faith is patience. Faith produces in us the ability to gracefully wait and move through life effortless. Walking in patience should be our emotional disposition as we await the manifestation of God's promises in our lives. We all must wait when we are in faith, but we do not have to be patient. Patience is a choice. It is taking a position of rest as we wait. It's knowing our turn will come, that we will be taking care of. It is knowing we have not been forgotten or looked over. Patience stems from knowing we already have spiritual ownership of what we are waiting to physically possess.

Hebrews 6:11-12 AMPC "But we do [[a]strongly and earnestly] desire for each of you to show the same diligence and sincerity [all the way through] in realizing and enjoying the full assurance and development of [your] hope until the end, In order that you may not grow disinterested and become [spiritual] sluggards, but imitators, behaving as do those who through faith ([b]by their leaning of the entire personality on God in Christ in absolute trust and confidence in His power, wisdom, and goodness) and by practice of patient endurance and waiting are [now] inheriting the promises."

We rest in the assurance of God's love for us while we are standing in faith. His integrity and character are sure. He will fulfill His Word. Knowing this causes us to be fully persuaded what He has promised is already performed in the spiritual realm where He abides. We are simply waiting in faith and patience for the manifestation of the promises of God in our lives. All believers must wait at some point in their faith walk. We now can exercise our patience as we await the manifestation of His Word. Faith and patience go hand in hand. If we are truly in faith, we also have patience. How long are we to remain in faith? Until it manifests! Faith does not have a time limit or an expiration date. Faith does not have a Plan B or back up plan. Faith does not pitch a fit or have a pity party because of delayed manifestation. Faith does NOT anticipate failure; therefore, faith does not get mad, take its toys and go home when things do not go as we have planned.

It is impossible to obtain the promises of God without having both faith and patience. As we wait, we must lean, put all the weight of our trust and confidence in our Father God's power, wisdom, and goodness. Through faith and patience, those who walked in faith before us awaited the manifestation of what they were hoping for. They are wonderful examples for us to imitate. They have demonstrated to us how they obtained the promises of God through faith and patience.

Hebrews 11:2-4 AMPC "For by [faith—[a]trust and holy fervor born of faith] the men of old had divine testimony borne to them and obtained a good report. By faith we understand that the worlds [during the successive ages] were framed (fashioned, put in order, and equipped for their intended purpose) by the word of God, so that what we see was not made from things which are visible."

Possessing faith is not denying problems or issues that may currently exist in our lives. It is however, denying they have a right to stay. What we are dealing with may be a fact or our current reality. However; as believers, we have the right to declare or speak about things that do not physically exist as though they do. NOW, faith is the ability to remain fixed on the truth of God's Word until what we see in the natural looks like what we are beholding in the spirit. Faith is choosing to allow the Word of God to take precedence in our lives over natural situations. It allows us to perceive as reality what is not visible to the senses.

Faith is what every believer must use to obtain a good outcome regarding our relationships, health, finances, etc. The miracles and testimonies we now see were not made by things that are do appear. They are a result of NOW faith. We will have what we say. Therefore, we must continually call those things that are not as though they are. Now, faith IS!

CHAPTER SEVEN FAITH NOTES

CONCLUSION

"Leap and the net will appear" John Burroughs

Faith is a beautiful gift given to the believer by the Father. It equips us with the courage to leap when we don't see a net or where we will land before we jump. Faith is not stepping out on nothing. Faith is stepping out on a Word from God. My prayer is that Faith 101 has encouraged and strengthened you in your walk of Faith.

I pray Faith has been simplified in your mind and therefore made more accessible to you. Faith encompasses everything we need to navigate victoriously through life, and I am honored to be a small part of helping you to understand more about the faith you already possess.

If this book has blessed you, please let me know by emailing me at getyourmindright247@gmail.com or writing me: Angela J. Walker, % Deliverance Family Worship Center, 406 Scott Street, Jonesboro AR 72401. I look forward to hearing from you. Blessings!

ABOUT THE AUTHOR

Angela J. Walker is an author, motivational speaker, life coach, teacher and honorably discharged army veteran. More importantly to Angela, she is a wife, mother, and grandmother. By faith Angela is boldly walking out the plan of God for her life. Angela's passion is sharing the simplicity of the Word of God through her books and teachings. Angela's goal is to help believers to better understand the power of the faith they already possess and encourage them to trust God more. Angela has been in ministry for over 30 years. She currently leads the women's ministry of her church Deliverance Family Worship Center, which she co-founded with her husband in 2000. Angela has been married for 33 years, she has three adult children, a daughter in love and two beautiful grandchildren.

INFORMATION FOR SPEAKING ENGAGEMENT

Angela J. Walker
c/o Deliverance Family Worship Center
406 Scott Street
Jonesboro, AR 72401
(870) 931-5453
angela.walker@dfwc.org
getyourmindright247@gmail.com

Other Books by Angela

Get Your Mind Right

Who Am I? Understanding My Identity In Christ
\

Made in the USA
Columbia, SC
14 August 2024

39988386R00062